Gathering

Gathering

A Northwoods Counting Book

Betsy Bowen

Houghton Mifflin Company
Boston 1999

Zero degrees

It's springtime in the northwoods. Winter seems a long way off. But in only a few months, the temperature will be down to zero, the lakes frozen, the flowers and leaves gone, and the bears and skunks asleep in their dens. So all through the warm, bright days of summer and the crisp, clear days of fall, we'll gather food and firewood and memories to be ready for the white snow and the cold, dark nights when they come.

0

MAY

One seed

In late May, we start planting. Each vegetable in the garden starts with just one seed. It takes a long time to tend and grow the food we'll need to last through the winter: tomatoes and beans for canning, plus piles of carrots, potatoes, rutabagas, and squash. In February, when we eat the vegetables we've grown, they will have the fresh taste of summer and they will smell like the earth.

1

MAY

Two rhubarb pies

Every year the bright red rhubarb stalks, with their big curled leaves, come up by themselves. We never have to replant. By June the plants are huge. Sometimes when we go to pick, we spot toads living in the dark, cool spaces under the leaves. There's so much rhubarb, we make two pies right away, then put the extra in the freezer to make into jam and cakes and more pies during the winter.

2

JUNE

Three summer memories

Summer is the time to let loose in the northwoods. It is the shortest of all the seasons, and we need to collect lots of warm memories to make it through the long, cold winter. By July we already have three especially good ones tucked away: floating along in the canoes under shooting stars, jumping off the cliff into the river, and catching a whole jarful of blinking fireflies.

3

JULY

Four bears

The animals here spend the warm months preparing for winter, too. Bears get ready by fattening up on berries and plants and grubs. We see four of them one afternoon, a mother and three cubs, eating raspberries in the woods. They have to eat now, because their food will be gone when the snow comes, and the bears must be fat enough to keep their big bodies warm during their winter sleep.

4

JULY

Five blueberries

Five blueberries isn't many to put away for winter, but that's all the littlest helper has in his tub because he keeps eating them — they're so ripe and sweet and warm from the sun. We'll put most of the berries in the freezer for later — to make into pancakes and muffins and pies. Some we make into jam with the rhubarb, and then we call it *bluebarb*. On snowy mornings, we'll pack frozen berries in our lunches; by noontime they are thawed and ready to eat. Yum!

5

AUGUST

Six bags of wild rice

When the wild rice ripens in September, we drop everything and go. We paddle to the marshy place in the lake where it grows, and whack it with sticks so the seeds fall into the bottom of the empty canoe. Later, we'll take the grain to be parched. We're hoping for six bags full, enough to cook for special dinners when visitors come, and some extra for hot, steaming winter soup. Wild rice is called *mahnomin* by the Ojibwe people here. They honor it as a gift to them from the Creator.

6

SEPTEMBER

Seven walleyes

On the last fishing trip of the season, we catch seven walleyes. The biggest weighs five pounds, a nice one to save in the freezer for Thanksgiving. We don't get any mosquito bites this trip; the chilly fall air has driven away the bugs. A few orange maple leaves are floating on the lake as we reel in. Time to put away the boat until next spring.

7

MN8585EY

SEPTEMBER

Eight
cords of
wood

On a blue-sky day in fall, our firewood arrives — eight cords of birch logs, enough to last this year and next. To make sure the chimney will be safe all season, the chimney sweep comes to clean it in his tall stovepipe hat. The wood burning in the warm winter stove will keep away the cold.

8

OCTOBER

Nine extension cords

The first snow turned the ground white for a few hours today. With the colder temperatures, the truck is a little slow to start, and we know that when the thermometer drops below zero, it won't start at all unless we plug it in. So we lay out nine extension cords end to end, to reach all the way from the house down the path to the truck. To help us see where to walk in the winter dark, we hang Christmas lights in the trees along the way. When a fresh snowfall covers them up, the snow will glow pink and blue and yellow.

9

OCTOBER

Ten skis

After we pull out all of the winter hats, mittens, coats, and boots, then find the snow shovels and fix the sleds, the last thing to get ready is our skis, all ten of them. We wax the bottoms and check to see who has grown out of last year's pair; we'll take the ones that are too short to the ski swap to trade. With the leaves off the trees now, we can see a long way through the woods. Soon the bigger snowfalls will come, and we'll have enough snow to ski on the trails back there.

10

NOVEMBER

Eleven
friends

The season of chores is over now, so eleven good friends come for a feast. We gather around the table to eat garden beans and squash, stuffed walleye, wild rice, and blueberry pie for dessert. Someone saw a woolly-bear caterpillar today with a wide yellow stripe — that means a hard winter for sure. But we can't wait to ski, skate, and fish through the ice. We're ready now — let winter come!

11

NOVEMBER

Twelve inches

This morning, snowflakes started falling fast and thick from the soft gray sky. The buses took all the kids home early from school. So far the snow is twelve inches deep. Tomorrow we'll be able to ski!

12

DECEMBER

All day long

. . . we ski on the fresh snow; we find our familiar trails and discover some new ones, too. Tonight we'll gather around the fire to thaw our feet and drink hot cider. We're settled in for winter now. Before long, we'll count the days until spring.

In honor of teachers,
enthusiastic and caring,
in particular,
Miss Glixon,
who taught me
to measure
the sun passing across the floor
through the seasons
of fourth grade.

Thanks to Jeremy Bowen for his careful attention
and craftsmanship in the color woodblock printing.

Library of Congress Cataloging-in-Publication Data

Bowen, Betsy.
Gathering: a northwoods counting book / Betsy Bowen.
p.   cm.
RNF ISBN 0-395-98133-6 PAP ISBN 0-395-98134-4
1. Counting — Juvenile literature. 2. Natural history —
Minnesota — Juvenile literature. 3. Seasons — Minnesota —
Juvenile literature. [1. Natural history — Minnesota. 2.
Country life — Minnesota. 3. Seasons. 4. Counting.] 1. Title.
QA113.B683   1995
513.2′11 — DC20
[E]   94-34491

The pictures in this book are woodblock prints, made by
carving the design and the big letters and numbers, backwards,
into flat blocks of white pine. One piece of wood is used for
each color, inked and printed by hand on a Vandercook No. 4
letterpress housed at the historic Grand Marais Art Colony.

Manufactured in Singapore
TWP 10 9 8 7 6 5 4 3 2 1

CONTENTS

CANDLEWICK PRESS
CAMBRIDGE, MASSACHUSETTS

SEEING STARS

James Muirden

1 Galileo Galilei was born in 1564 in a town called Pisa, in northern Italy. He grew up to make important discoveries about the things we see in the night sky.

2 No one knows who actually invented the telescope, but in 1609 Galileo found out that a Dutchman named Hans Lippershey had made one. Galileo then had the bright idea of using one to look into space.

3 Through his telescope, Galileo discovered four of Jupiter's 16 moons. He also spotted thousands of stars that no one had seen before.

4

What really caused a stir was when Galileo claimed that the earth traveled around the sun. In those days nearly everyone else believed it was the other way around—that the sun traveled around the earth.

5 Galileo's ideas were considered so dangerous that he was locked in his home to keep him from spreading them. This didn't stop Galileo from carrying on his work, though, and he continued studying and writing about space until his death, in 1642.

CONTENTS

CANDLEWICK PRESS
CAMBRIDGE, MASSACHUSETTS

SEEING STARS

James Muirden

1 Galileo Galilei was born in 1564 in a town called Pisa, in northern Italy. He grew up to make important discoveries about the things we see in the night sky.

2 No one knows who actually invented the telescope, but in 1609 Galileo found out that a Dutchman named Hans Lippershey had made one. Galileo then had the bright idea of using one to look into space.

3 Through his telescope, Galileo discovered four of Jupiter's 16 moons. He also spotted thousands of stars that no one had seen before.

4

What really caused a stir was when Galileo claimed that the earth traveled around the sun. In those days nearly everyone else believed it was the other way around—that the sun traveled around the earth.

5 Galileo's ideas were considered so dangerous that he was locked in his home to keep him from spreading them. This didn't stop Galileo from carrying on his work, though, and he continued studying and writing about space until his death, in 1642.

STARRY, STARRY NIGHT

1 Have you ever tried to count the stars? On dark nights you can see hundreds. There are lots more you can't see, though, because they're so faint they can be found only by using a telescope.

2 Astronomers are people who study the stars. They think there may be a hundred million million million stars altogether— that's 100,000,000,000,000,000,000!

3 Stars look tiny from Earth. But if you could visit one, this is the sort of thing you'd find . . .

4 a vast, scorching-hot ball of glowing gas—much like our sun, because the sun is actually our nearest star!

5 The sun may be a close neighbor, but it's still 93 million miles away from us. It would take about 150 years to travel that far in a car!

6 We'd all be frizzled if the sun were any nearer, though, because it gives off as much heat as 1,000 million million million million electric fires all switched on at once. Temperatures at the center of the sun are about 27 million°F.

4 STARS

7 The sun is dazzlingly bright, too. You should NEVER look directly at it, in fact, because its light is so strong it could harm your eyes, even on hazy days.

8 Even so, the sun isn't particularly hot or bright compared with other stars. And although a million Earths could fit inside it, it isn't all that big either.

9 Some of those tiny twinkling lights you see on starry nights are gigantic—big enough for a million stars like our sun to fit inside them!

STAR PICTURES

1 Meet Orion, the hunter. He's a constellation, a group of stars that makes a picture—that is, if you connect the stars like a dot-to-dot drawing and use a lot of imagination!

2 We don't know who first drew constellations, but we do know it was happening 5,000 years ago in the area we now call the Middle East.

3 Back in ancient times, people made up stories to explain where the stars came from.

4 Orion was first drawn by the ancient Greeks. In their stories he was a giant who could walk on water.

6 CONSTELLATIONS

5 The Greeks believed that after Orion died, their gods put him in the sky, where he's fighting a constellation called Taurus, the bull.

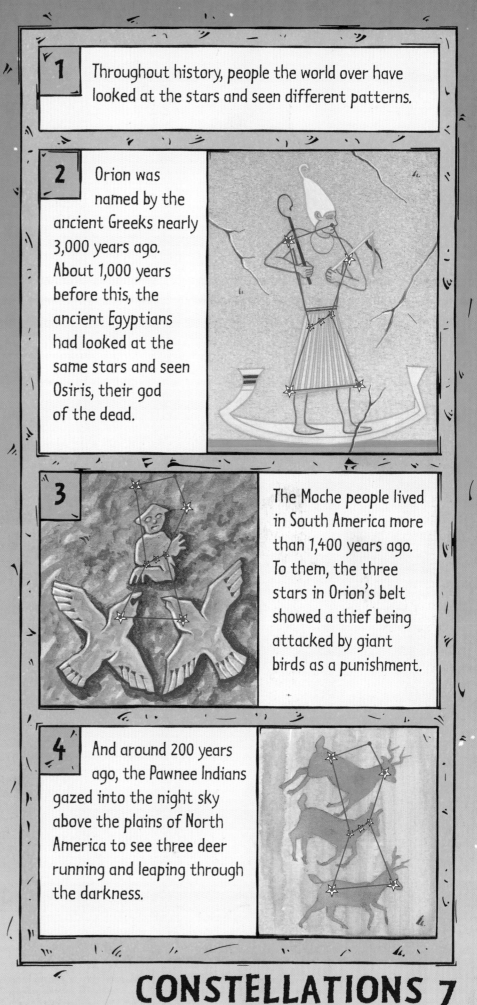

6 Picking out a constellation is never easy. You won't be able to see Orion every night, but he is one of the clearest—look for the three bright stars that make up his belt.

1 Throughout history, people the world over have looked at the stars and seen different patterns.

2 Orion was named by the ancient Greeks nearly 3,000 years ago. About 1,000 years before this, the ancient Egyptians had looked at the same stars and seen Osiris, their god of the dead.

3 The Moche people lived in South America more than 1,400 years ago. To them, the three stars in Orion's belt showed a thief being attacked by giant birds as a punishment.

4 And around 200 years ago, the Pawnee Indians gazed into the night sky above the plains of North America to see three deer running and leaping through the darkness.

GUIDED BY THE LIGHT

1 Navigating means keeping track of where you are and in which direction you're going, so it's very important when you're traveling.

2 For thousands of years, travelers have used the constellations as signposts to help them navigate.

3 Two constellations are particularly useful because they help us find the north and the south.

4 The Little Bear constellation points toward the north, while the Southern Cross constellation is used to find the south.

5 Each constellation is a bit like a compass in the sky, since if you know where north or south is, you can figure out other directions, too.

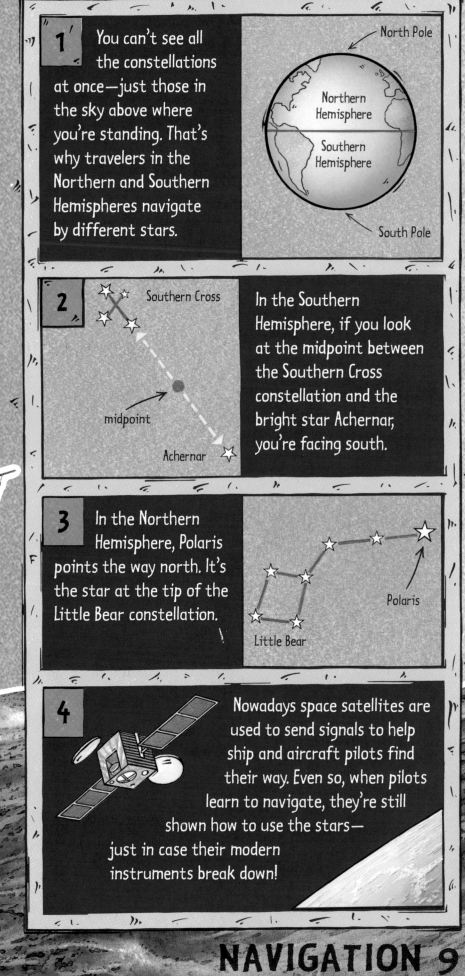

1 You can't see all the constellations at once—just those in the sky above where you're standing. That's why travelers in the Northern and Southern Hemispheres navigate by different stars.

North Pole

Northern Hemisphere

Southern Hemisphere

South Pole

2 Southern Cross

midpoint

Achernar

In the Southern Hemisphere, if you look at the midpoint between the Southern Cross constellation and the bright star Achernar, you're facing south.

3 In the Northern Hemisphere, Polaris points the way north. It's the star at the tip of the Little Bear constellation.

Polaris

Little Bear

4 Nowadays space satellites are used to send signals to help ship and aircraft pilots find their way. Even so, when pilots learn to navigate, they're still shown how to use the stars—just in case their modern instruments break down!

SPACE FAKES

2 Real stars are made from gas. But comets are mountain-sized lumps of snow and dust—more like gigantic dirty snowballs than stars!

1 From time to time a strange "star" shines in the night sky, only to disappear a few weeks later. It's not really a star, of course, it's a comet.

1 Here's another kind of fake star. Many people call it a "shooting star," but its real name is a meteor.

2 Meteors start off as pea-sized pieces of space rock. They're so small that hundreds could fit inside an astronaut's pocket!

10 COMETS

3 Comets are space travelers that journey around and around our star, the sun. At times they're very close to the sun, but at others they're millions of miles away.

4 Comets may look bright, but unlike stars they don't make their own light. We can see comets only when they come close enough to the sun for its light to shine on them.

5 When a comet does get close to the sun, its snow becomes boiling hot and turns into a gassy cloud. This streams out behind the hurtling comet and is called its tail.

3 When pieces of space rock hurtle through the air around Earth, they burn up and vanish. From the ground they look like bright lights streaking across the night sky, and these flashes of light are what we call meteors.

4 Some people believe that you should make a wish if you spot a shooting star. But it'll be gone in a flash, so you'll have to be quick!

METEORS 11

A STAR IS BORN

1 Did you know that the stars you see in the night sky weren't always there and that a new star is born somewhere in space every year?

2 Stars begin their lives inside a nebula— a vast, dark cloud of dust and gas.

3 Every now and then, big clumps of dust and gas start whirling around inside the nebula, spinning faster all the time.

4 Astronomers call these clumps protostars, which means "not-yet-stars." Over time, a single nebula may give birth to thousands of them.

12 NEBULAE

5 As each protostar spins, its dust and gas are pulled inward into a ball. The protostar gets hotter, too, until it begins to glow.

6 Slowly the protostar grows hotter and brighter—until one night, millions of years later, a newborn star is sparkling and twinkling in the sky.

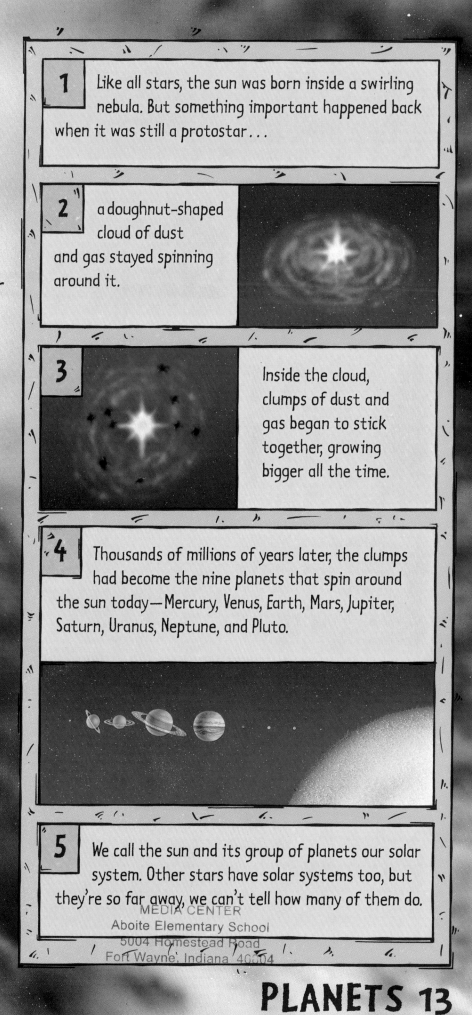

1 Like all stars, the sun was born inside a swirling nebula. But something important happened back when it was still a protostar...

2 a doughnut-shaped cloud of dust and gas stayed spinning around it.

3 Inside the cloud, clumps of dust and gas began to stick together, growing bigger all the time.

4 Thousands of millions of years later, the clumps had become the nine planets that spin around the sun today—Mercury, Venus, Earth, Mars, Jupiter, Saturn, Uranus, Neptune, and Pluto.

5 We call the sun and its group of planets our solar system. Other stars have solar systems too, but they're so far away, we can't tell how many of them do.

1   Imagining the different brightnesses of stars is difficult, but one helpful way is to compare them with lights on Earth.

2   A medium-sized star, like the sun, gives off a strong yellow-white light. Think of it shining like the bright electric bulb in a desk lamp.

3   If the sun shines like a desk lamp, a red dwarf's faint ruby glow is no stronger than the light given off by the on button on a television set.

4   But blue giants are so huge and so hot that they beam out like a lighthouse, putting every other star in the shade!

1   Most stars look fairly alike from Earth, but if you could travel out to them, you'd see they come in different sizes and shine with different colors and brightnesses, too.

2   The smallest and dimmest stars are called dwarfs. The largest and brightest are called giants. And in between there are medium-sized stars, like the sun.

14 STAR BRIGHTNESS

DWARFS AND GIANTS

3 Red dwarfs glimmer faintly with a dull reddish glow. They reach temperatures of 5,400°F—which may sound like a lot, but is cool for a star.

4 Medium-sized stars are about ten times the diameter, or width, of a red dwarf. They're twice as hot, too, and their starlight is yellow and bright.

5 Blue giants are the real superstars, though! At up to ten times the diameter of the sun, they glare out 100,000 times more fiercely, with a dazzling bluish white light.

STAR BRIGHTNESS 15

DOUBLE DAZZLERS

1 New stars are born together in big families called clusters. Then as they get older, most of them drift away to shine on their own.

2 But about a quarter of all stars are born as twins and stay together all their lives. They're called binary stars—"bi" means two, as in the word "bicycle."

3 Everything in space travels around its own invisible pathway called an orbit. The moon travels around Earth, for example, while Earth travels around the sun.

1 What is the pulling force we call gravity like? We can't see it, but we'd know if it weren't there. Without the earth's gravity tugging downward, everything would float off into space, like lost balloons.

4 Binary stars spend their whole lives traveling around each other. This is because each star's pulling force—its gravity—is strong enough to keep them together.

5 Some binary stars are very close and orbit each other in hours. But others are so far apart that a single orbit can take thousands of years!

2 It's the earth's gravity that holds the moon in orbit around us, too. It's like an invisible piece of string keeping the moon from flying away.

3 Everything in space has gravity. The more massive it is, the stronger its gravity. The sun is so much more massive than the earth that its gravity is powerful enough to keep all nine planets and their moons orbiting around it.

THE MILKY WAY

1 All the stars you see at night are just a tiny part of a vast starry grouping called a galaxy.

2 There are lots of galaxies in space. We call ours the Milky Way, and this is what it looks like from above. Our sun is just a dot about a third of the way in from the edge.

3 Astronomers think there are at least 200 billion stars in the Milky Way. But don't start counting them—it would take you well over 60,000 years!

18 GALAXIES

4 Like everything else in space, the Milky Way is swirling around and around. It isn't moving very quickly, though.

5 The whole thing turns so slowly that it has spun around only once since the first dinosaurs lived on Earth, 220 million years ago!

1 Galaxies come in different sizes, just as stars do, and there are also three basic types.

2 Many are shaped like the Milky Way, with their stars swirling and spiraling out from the center. That's why they're called spiral galaxies.

They look like spirals only from above, though. From the side, they're more like flying saucers!

3 In elliptical galaxies, the stars form an egg shape—an ellipse is a kind of oval shape.

4 And then there are the irregular galaxies—"irregular" means uneven, with no special shape at all.

When it comes to names, galaxies are given letters and numbers, such as M33 and NGC 1275. But some also have nicknames. For example, there's a strange pair of spiral galaxies known as the Mice. They were given this name because each one looks as if it has a tail.

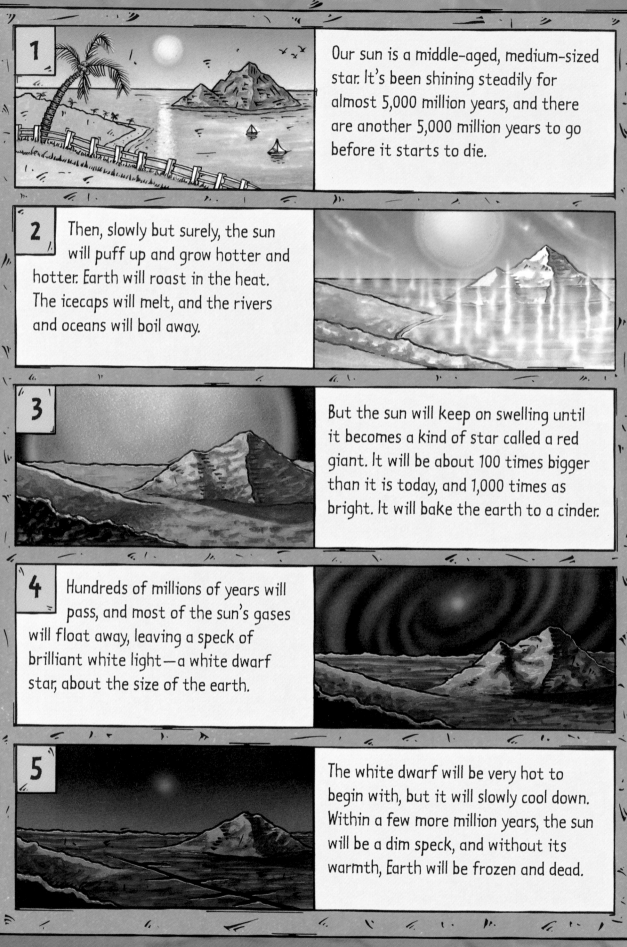

1 Our sun is a middle-aged, medium-sized star. It's been shining steadily for almost 5,000 million years, and there are another 5,000 million years to go before it starts to die.

2 Then, slowly but surely, the sun will puff up and grow hotter and hotter. Earth will roast in the heat. The icecaps will melt, and the rivers and oceans will boil away.

3 But the sun will keep on swelling until it becomes a kind of star called a red giant. It will be about 100 times bigger than it is today, and 1,000 times as bright. It will bake the earth to a cinder.

4 Hundreds of millions of years will pass, and most of the sun's gases will float away, leaving a speck of brilliant white light—a white dwarf star, about the size of the earth.

5 The white dwarf will be very hot to begin with, but it will slowly cool down. Within a few more million years, the sun will be a dim speck, and without its warmth, Earth will be frozen and dead.

20 STAR DEATH

OUT WITH A BANG

1 Nothing lasts forever, not even a star. But just as stars look different from one another, so are their endings different, too.

2 A blue giant, for example, shines only for a few million years before starting to die.

3 Then it starts to overheat, puffing up like a balloon, until it grows into an enormous kind of star called a red supergiant.

4 The supergiant goes on, getting hotter and hotter and hotter, until . . .

BANG

5 The supergiant blows up like an immense bomb, hurling gas and dust out into space at speeds of more than 6,000 miles per second!

22 SUPERNOVAS

8 When the light at last fades away, something strange is left behind— a solid ball, only a few miles wide.

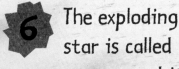 The exploding star is called a supernova, and it's the most spectacular light show in space.

9 It's called a neutron star. It doesn't shine, but it's scorching hot and unbelievably heavy. A piece the size of a grain of rice would weigh 110,000 tons, as much as a fully laden supertanker ship.

 7 It's as blinding as a billion suns. And although the blast is over within seconds, the supernova blazes for weeks—or even months.

10 Astronomers haven't seen a supernova in our galaxy for nearly 400 years, but they believe that one explodes somewhere in space every day. So, who knows, you could be lucky enough to see one tomorrow!

SUPERNOVAS 23

INDEX

Main illustrations by Christian Hook (6); Lawrie Taylor (3);
Ian Thompson (cover, 4–5, 10–19, 21–23); Peter Visscher (8–9)
Inset and picture-strip illustrations by Ian Thompson
With thanks to Bernard Thornton Artists and Claire Llewellyn
Designed by Matthew Lilly and Tiffany Leeson; edited by Paul Harrison
Consultant: Carole Stott
Text copyright © 1998 by James Muirden
Illustrations copyright © 1998 by Walker Books Ltd.
All rights reserved. First U.S. edition 1998
Library of Congress Cataloging-in-Publication Data is available.
Library of Congress Catalog Card Number 97-32577
ISBN 0-7636-0373-2 (hardcover)
ISBN 0-7636-0647-2 (paperback)
2 4 6 8 10 9 7 5 3 1
Printed in Hong Kong
This book was typeset in Kosmik.
Candlewick Press
2067 Massachusetts Avenue
Cambridge, Massachusetts 02140

QUIZ ANSWERS

Page 2—FALSE
The center of a star is the hottest part.
The surface temperature of the sun reaches
about 11,000°F, for example, but at the
center, the temperature can be 27,000,000°F.

Page 6—FALSE
There are 88 constellations now, but
there used to be many more. In 1922, an
international committee of astronomers
agreed there were too many and cut the
list down to the present number.

Page 8—TRUE
Scientists believe that some birds, such
as blackcaps, use the stars to guide them
when they fly south, away from the cold
northern winters.

Page 11—TRUE
Meteor showers are quite common.
Most are caused by pieces of dust
given off by passing comets.

Page 12—FALSE
Some scientists think that only about
a quarter of all stars have planets.

Page 15—TRUE
Some astronomers believe that just
over a third of all stars are red dwarfs.

Page 17—FALSE
Very often, one of the binary stars
is much brighter than the other.

Page 18—FALSE
Astronomers believe that the Milky Way
is one of the biggest galaxies in space.

Page 20—TRUE
The gas from a dying star floats away
and eventually forms a nebula cloud.